Dear Parents:

Congratulations! Your child is taking
the first steps on an exciting journey.
The destination? Independent reading!

STEP INTO READING® will help your child get there. The program offers
five steps to reading success. Each step includes fun stories and colorful
art or photographs. In addition to original fiction and books with favorite
characters, there are Step into Reading Non-Fiction Readers, Phonics Readers
and Boxed Sets, Sticker Readers, and Comic Readers—a complete literacy
program with something to interest every child.

Learning to Read, Step by Step!

 Ready to Read   Preschool–Kindergarten
• big type and easy words • rhyme and rhythm • picture clues
For children who know the alphabet and are eager to
begin reading.

 Reading with Help   Preschool–Grade 1
• basic vocabulary • short sentences • simple stories
For children who recognize familiar words and sound out
new words with help.

 Reading on Your Own   Grades 1–3
• engaging characters • easy-to-follow plots • popular topics
For children who are ready to read on their own.

 Reading Paragraphs   Grades 2–3
• challenging vocabulary • short paragraphs • exciting stories
For newly independent readers who read simple sentences
with confidence.

 Ready for Chapters   Grades 2–4
• chapters • longer paragraphs • full-color art
For children who want to take the plunge into chapter books
but still like colorful pictures.

STEP INTO READING® is designed to give every child a successful
reading experience. The grade levels are only guides; children will progress
through the steps at their own speed, developing confidence in their reading.

Remember, a lifetime love of reading starts with a single step!

For Jacob
—N.E.

Special thanks to Sherin Kwan and Alex Wiltshire

All rights reserved. Published in the United States by Random House Children's Books, a division of Penguin Random House LLC, 1745 Broadway, New York, NY 10019, and in Canada by Penguin Random House Canada Limited, Toronto.

Step into Reading, Random House, and the Random House colophon are registered trademarks of Penguin Random House LLC.

Visit us on the Web!
StepIntoReading.com
rhcbooks.com
minecraft.net
Educators and librarians, for a variety of teaching tools, visit us at RHTeachersLibrarians.com

ISBN 978-0-593-48304-6 (trade) — ISBN 978-0-593-48305-3 (lib. bdg.) —
ISBN 978-0-593-48306-0 (ebook)

Printed in the United States of America
10 9 8 7 6 5 4 3 2 1

THE SKY's THE LIMIT!

by Nick Eliopulos

illustrated by Alan Batson

Random House 🏠 New York

Emmy and Birch
were jumping on their beds,
trying to decide what
their next adventure
in the world of
Minecraft would be.

Jumping on beds was fun.
Birch said he wanted
to go even higher.
"I have an idea,"
said Emmy.

Emmy's idea
was to gather
sixteen slime blocks.
She set them on the ground
like a great green trampoline.

Emmy jumped first.

She hit the trampoline

and bounced into the air!

Seeing that it was safe,

Birch jumped, too.

Emmy and Birch

bounced higher—

higher than ever before!

But it was not high
enough for Birch.
He wanted to fly
like a parrot.
"I have another idea,"
said Emmy.

In her room,

Emmy had a treasure chest.

Inside the chest,

she kept all her

strange and marvelous

Minecraft loot.

At last, Emmy found
what she was looking for.
She showed Birch
a pair of wings
called elytra.
"With these on your back,
you will be able to fly,"
she said.

Birch put on the wings

right away.

He was very excited to fly!

He leaped off the cliff

before Emmy could warn him that

there was a problem . . .

The elytra were old
and broken.
They did not work.

Emmy knew how to fix the wings.
They would need to find
a phantom and stay awake
for three days!
Silly Birch thought smashing
their beds would do the trick!

To stay awake,
Emmy and Birch
went on an adventure
underground. Together,
they fought hostile mobs
in a mossy cave.

Emmy blocked arrows

with her shield

while Birch defeated creepers

before they could explode.

Byte made sure

any cute animal mobs

were safe from harm.

On their second night
without sleep,
they climbed back up
to the surface.
In a creepy swamp,
they fought slimes
in the mud.

Despite the battle,
Emmy was able to add
some blue orchids
from the swamp
to the other flowers
in her inventory.

On their third night,

Emmy used a crafting table

to make fireworks

out of gunpowder and paper.

Birch used a furnace
to cook steaks.
He gave the first steak
to Byte.
The tame wolf
loved it.

After their picnic,
Emmy and Birch
looked up at the stars.
It was a clear night,
with a bright full moon.

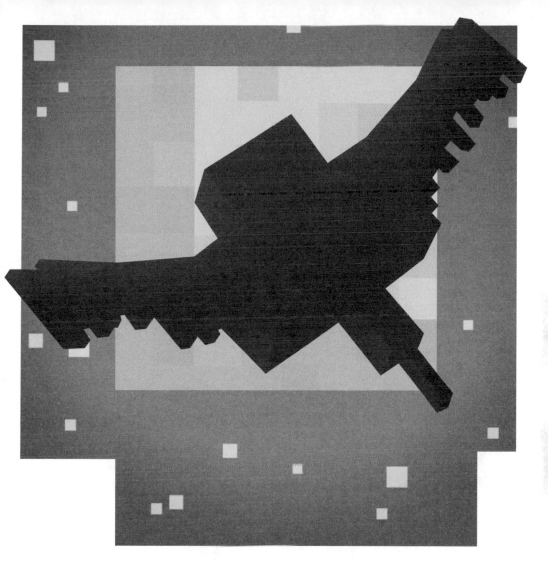

Suddenly, Birch saw something
fly across the moon.
"Is it a bird?" he asked.
"Or is it a bat?"

"That's a phantom!"
Emmy shouted.
The hostile mob swooped
down at them.

The phantom attacked
again and again!
It was fast and silent—
and scary!

Birch swung his sword.
Emmy fired an arrow
with her bow.
Working together,
they defeated the phantom.

The phantom left behind
a little piece of itself.
The piece was called
a phantom membrane.

At an anvil,
Emmy used
the phantom membrane
to fix the old elytra.

Finally,

Birch was able to fly!

He glided through the air.

Emmy cheered.

Byte wagged his tail.

A parrot squawked in surprise!

Birch used his elytra
and a firework rocket
to soar higher and higher.
From so far up,
he could see
all across the Overworld.

There was an ocean
they could swim in,
a mountain
they could climb,
and a desert pyramid
they had yet to explore.

Birch told Emmy about
everything he had seen.
"Are you ready
for another adventure?"
he asked.
"Always!" said Emmy. "Let's go!"